Bright **Summaries**.com

The Lady of the Camellias

by Alexandre Dumas fils

The Lady of the Camellias

BY ALEXANDRE DUMAS FILS

ALEXANDRE DUMAS FILS

FRENCH WRITER

- **Born in 1824 in Paris**

- **Died in 1895 at Marly-le-Roi**

- **Some of his works:**

  - *The Clemenceau Affair, Memoir of the Accused* (1866), novel

  - *Le Fils naturel* (1858), play

  - *Un père prodigue* (1859), play

Alexandre Dumas fils bears the same name as his father, the famous author of The *Three Musketeers*. With *La Dame aux camélias*, published in 1848, he distinguished himself as a talented writer and stepped out of his father's shadow. During his lifetime he was mainly known for his theatrical works, although he also wrote numerous novels. His work is characterised by a well-crafted style and witty, sharp sentences, particularly suitable for the theatre. He was very close to realism in literature. His work is distinguished by its moralistic character and its criticism of his time.

THE LADY OF THE CAMELLIAS

THE IMPOSSIBLE LOVE OF A PARISIAN COURTESAN IN THE 19TH CENTURY

- **Genre:** novel

- **Reference edition**: *La Dame aux camélias*, Paris, Le Livre de Poche, 1975, 285 p.

- **1st edition:** 1848

- **Themes:** love, realism, Parisian life, 19th century, courtesans, jealousy

The Lady of the Camellias was written by Alexandre Dumas fils after the death of his former mistress and first love, Marie Duplessis, a prominent courtesan in Paris in the mid-1800s. This novel, considered one of the precursors of realism, was adapted for the stage by the author himself. It has become a classic of literature and has been adapted in many forms (opera, film, ballet). The novel depicts the love affair between Armand Duval, a passionate young man, and Marguerite Duval, a 'kept woman'. Their relationship is compromised by Marguerite's past, which constantly catches up with them, either through Armand's jealousy or through the disapproval of his father.

SUMMARY

ALEXANDRE DUMAS MEETS ARMAND DUVAL

The story begins in Paris in 1847. In the first chapters, Alexandre Dumas fils is the narrator. He tells of how he learned of the death of a famous courtesan, Marguerite Gautier. The woman died riddled with debts, and an auction of her personal belongings was organised. The narrator goes there to attend the event. Many ladies of the 'Tout-Paris', nobles and respectable bourgeois, are present. They come out of curiosity, to get a glimpse of the scandalous lifestyle of a 'maintained' woman, and in the hope of being able to take possession of one of the many luxury items that Marguerite Gautier's lovers have given her during her life. Alexandre Dumas buys a book, *Manon Lescaut*, at a high price, in which there is a note from a certain Armand Duval.

Later, Alexandre Dumas fils meets Armand Duval, who comes to Dumas' house to buy the book that he had given to the deceased Marguerite Gautier. The two young men become friends and Dumas learns that Armand Duval had been one of Marguerite Gautier's many lovers. The latter seems particularly affected by the death of his former mistress. He explains to Alexandre Dumas fils that he intends to buy a perpetual plot for her in the Montmartre cemetery. In fact, this was the only way he could see her corpse. He was absent at the time of her death and needs to see her lifeless body to mourn.

Armand Duval finally manages to see the already decomposing corpse of his former lover. The shock makes him seriously ill, and Alexandre Dumas fils keeps watch at his bedside. It is then that Armand Duval starts to tell him about his love for the courtesan Marguerite Gautier, known in Paris as the Lady of the Camellias.

ARMAND DUVAL MEETS MARGUERITE GAUTIER

From that moment on, Armand Duval becomes the narrator of the story. The first time he meets Marguerite Gautier is while walking on the Place de la Bourse. He sees her enter a shop and is immediately struck by her grace and great beauty. He did not dare approach her. A few days later, on his way to the Opéra-Comique with a friend, Armand Duval saw Marguerite in a box opposite his own. He asks his friend, who knows the Lady of the Camellias, to introduce her to him. This first meeting does not go according to Armand's taste, since Marguerite gently mocks him and he makes a fool of himself, offended by this mockery. Nevertheless, Armand discreetly follows her after the performance to her front door. From that moment on, the young man develops an obsession with Marguerite, whom he often sees.

One day, Armand learns that she is ill with tuberculosis and he regularly asks for news from people who can give him information. Since the Lady of the Camellias was always on his mind, Armand decided to meet her again. One evening, at the Variétés theatre, he saw her in the company of a lady in her forties, a former courtesan named Prudence Duvernoy. He approaches her and learns that she is Marguerite Gautier's neighbour. Armand then asks her to introduce him to Marguerite. Prudence accepts and it is agreed that he and his friend Gaston, who accompanies him that evening, go together to Prudence's house. That evening, Marguerite Gautier receives a visit from one of her suitors, the Count of G., who annoys her terribly. She asks Prudence to join her at her house and agrees to let her come with her two guests. This is how Armand finds himself at Marguerite Gautier's house. After distinguishing himself to her with his wit, he tells her that he is the mysterious young man who has been checking on her regularly during her illness. During the course of the evening, he finally seduces her and confesses his feelings. The courtesan agrees to become his mistress and gives him a date for the next day.

ARMAND AND MARGUERITE BECOME LOVERS

Armand and Marguerite spend their first two nights of love together, but the young man finds it difficult to accept that his mistress is officially linked to a duke who maintains her and that the Count of G., her former lover, is still courting her assiduously. Prudence, Marguerite's friend and confidante, tries to reason with Armand: the young woman is a courtesan, offering herself to rich suitors in exchange for gifts, material benefits and money. For Prudence, Armand should expect nothing more than a passing affair, although Armand

and Marguerite are in love. But Armand is consumed with jealousy and on the third night, when he realises that Marguerite is spending the night with the Count of G., he decides to write an ironic and defamatory break-up letter to Marguerite, hoping for a response or reaction from her. Finally, when Marguerite does not reply, Armand, driven by pride and jealousy, decides to leave Paris and return to his father. But jealous as he is, he is no less madly in love and through Prudence, he writes a letter to Marguerite apologising. She shows up at his house just before Armand leaves Paris. Armand throws himself at Marguerite's feet to beg her forgiveness. When Armand explains his jealousy, Marguerite replies: "Well, my friend, you should have loved me a little less or understood me a little more" (p. 145). In the end, Marguerite forgives Armand for his jealousy, after explaining to him the obligations of a courtesan and reminding him of her love for him.

Armand decides to change his life and his way of seeing things in order to accept his mistress's scandalous life-style. He is consumed by love and has great difficulty in suppressing his jealousy. He begins to lead a hectic life-style, alternating between dates, parties, and gambling. He hardly sleeps and lives only for his passion with Marguerite. During a day spent in the countryside, the couple sees a house they like. Marguerite decides to ask the Duke, who is "protecting" her, to rent this house, under the pretext of getting away from the immoral life of Paris.

The Duke willingly agrees to rent the house in Bougival, seeing it as an opportunity to keep his protégée from a life of debauchery. But for Marguerite, it is a ploy to be able to live her relationship with Armand more freely. Eventually the Duke learns of the scandal and abandons Marguerite. The Lady of the Camellias has to give up the luxury to which she had become accustomed as a courtesan. She makes this sacrifice out of love for Armand and secretly sells her jewels and wealth to pay off the debts that have arisen after the Duke stops supporting her. Despite the money problems, Armand and Marguerite have a sincere love for each other and live the best days of their love in Bougival. They eventually promise each other a loyal love and decide to return to Paris to settle down together.

ARMAND'S FATHER INTERVENES

Then Armand's father arrives in Paris. He has learned of his son's relationship with a famous courtesan and intends to prevent it to preserve the family honour. At first he tries to dissuade Armand, but without success. One day when he returns from his father's house, Armand finds it empty. He goes in search of Marguerite and receives a letter from her telling him that she is cheating on him and that they must part. He is devastated by grief and leaves Paris to go to his father. Although he has recovered, he continues to think about Marguerite and decides to return to Paris. There he meets Marguerite again with another beautiful woman and decides to take revenge. He seduces Marguerite's wife, Olympe, and shows himself publicly with her. His relationship with Olympe saddens Marguerite greatly. Finally, she visits Armand and asks him to stop his cruel game. The young man then learns that Marguerite has fallen seriously ill again. They spend a night of love together, after which Marguerite promises Armand that she can always be his mistress, but not his companion. The next day, Armand tries to see Marguerite again, but she is with the Count of G. Mad with rage, he writes her an insulting letter and leaves for Egypt.

THE AGONY OF MARGUERITE

The rest of the story is not told by Armand. Alexandre Dumas fils tells us that the latter falls asleep after having entrusted the narrator with the diaries written by Marguerite after her departure, and which were entrusted to him after her death. In these diaries, Marguerite confides in Armand. She tells him the reason for their break-up: she had been visited by his father, who had convinced her to leave him for the sake of their family. Armand's love affair with a courtesan compromised his family's honour and prevented his sister from finding a husband. In the end, it was for love of Armand that Marguerite was persuaded to leave him. In the rest of the diary she describes her agony and doubts: suffering and lonely, she wonders where her lover is and wishes for his return, which she believes would facilitate her recovery. Above all, she hopes that he will forgive her for the pain she has caused him. Finally, Marguerite dies without seeing Armand again, still in Egypt.

CHARACTER STUDY

ARMAND DUVAL

Armand Duval, a passionate and emotional man, is the main character in this story, together with Marguerite Gautier. In the novel, he is the friend of Alexandre Dumas fils and the lover of the young girl. He is described as a young man in his twenties, tall, pale, and with blond hair. We can guess that he was sufficiently attractive to have attracted the attention of Marguerite Gautier, the Lady of the Camellias. When he meets Alexandre Dumas fils, while mourning his great love, Armand is literally sick with grief: he has a fever, cries constantly and faints several times. Born into a bourgeois provincial family, he has been sent to Paris by his father to train as a lawyer or doctor. He lives off his late mother's inheritance and a pension from his father. In Paris, he indulged in the social life, frequenting theatres and operas, where he met Marguerite Gautier. It was his mad love and his sincere concern for her health and happiness that seduced her. Armand is well aware that he is falling in love with a courtesan with a sulphurous past who is still seeing other lovers. However, he cannot come to terms with this and cannot help but feel a terrible jealousy. This jealousy, which he can never quite shake off, causes him a great deal of pain and forms the basis of his relationship with Marguerite, whose stability it constantly threatens. Indeed, it is jealousy that drives him to leave Marguerite the first time, and it is jealousy that makes him doubt Marguerite's desire to give up her life as a courtesan for him. Finally, it is jealousy and pride that drive him to make Marguerite suffer, and she cannot find the strength to fight both illness and sadness and finally succumbs.

Armand is also a loving and loyal son. When his father wants to oppose his relationship with Marguerite, Armand is overcome with doubt. Finally, he takes refuge at his father's house when he is the victim of his father's ploy to separate him from Marguerite.

MARGUERITE GAUTIER

Marguerite is described as a woman of exceptional beauty. She is tall and slim, with long black hair. Since Marguerite's beauty is one of the key elements of the novel, perhaps we should leave it to the author to describe her face, with his characteristic talent:

> "In an oval of indescribable grace, put black eyes surmounted by eyebrows of an arc so pure that it seemed painted; veil these eyes with large lashes which, when lowered, cast shadow on the pink tint of the cheeks; trace a fine, straight, spiritual nose, with nostrils a little opened by an ardent aspiration towards sensual life; Draw a regular mouth, whose lips opened gracefully over milk-white teeth; colour the skin with that velvetiness which covers peaches that no hand has touched, and you will have the whole of this charming head." (p.28)

Marguerite is a courtesan, a 'woman in care'. At that time, in the social circles of Paris, some women lived in contact with high society, from which they took lovers. They exchanged their graces for material benefits: gifts, but also money. This was not prostitution as we might hear it today: these women freely chose their lovers and did not charge for sexual services. Rather, it was a matter of self-interested love affairs. In this novel, Marguerite is the most coveted courtesan in Paris. She is nicknamed the Lady of the Camellias, because she is always adorned with these flowers. She differs from the other courtesans of her time by her greatness of spirit and her nobility. In the course of the novel, Marguerite falls in love with Armand Duval. She decides to abandon her life as a courtesan and sacrifice her fortune and future for Armand. In doing so, she reveals a loyalty and strength of will that no one suspected in a courtesan. Unfortunately, the reputation of a courtesan still pursues her. The social pressures of the time hinder her love for Armand. When Armand's father explains that Marguerite can only harm Armand by loving him, Marguerite is convinced. It is here that she makes the greatest sacrifice, which will cost her Armand's love and her life: she decides to renounce her love for Armand and to return to her life as a courtesan. She falls ill and dies of tuberculosis in bitter solitude.

PRUDENCE DUVERNOY

Prudence is Marguerite's neighbour and friend. She is a woman in her forties, a former courtesan who has lost her charms. At the time of the narrative, she is a milliner, but does not manage to sell many of her articles. In fact, she lives off Marguerite Gautier. Marguerite 'lends' her money which she never seeks to recover, buys her hats which she never wears and gives her gifts from her lovers which she is not interested in. Prudence is also Marguerite's confidante, and it is through her that Armand Duval manages to meet and seduce Marguerite Gautier. Despite Marguerite's generosity towards Prudence, the latter abandons her when Marguerite needs her most. Prudence stops seeing Marguerite when she is dying, debt-ridden and destitute. There is no physical description of Prudence, although we know that she is "fat" (p77). Prudence, like the other secondary characters in this novel, is a poorly developed character. With her sanctimonious speeches about the impossibility of loving a courtesan and her self-serving friendship, she serves mainly to highlight Marguerite Gautier's greatness of spirit, selfless generosity, and loving character.

M.DUVAL

Monsieur Duval is Armand's father. He arrives in Paris as soon as he learns of his son's love affair with a famous courtesan. He will do everything to oppose this relationship and preserve his family's honour. He wants to marry off his daughter and the groom's family refuses to accept the marriage, knowing that the bride's brother is having scandalous relations with a kept woman. He eventually convinces Marguerite to leave Armand, without the latter knowing about the scheme. No physical description is given of him, and the character is little developed in the novel. Monsieur Duval is the embodiment of the bourgeois morality of the time. Through him, the vocation to love and happiness of courtesans is challenged in the name of the moral values of the time. In the end, it is he who decides that a woman with too scandalous a past cannot experience the happiness of true love.

OLYMPE

Olympe is a courtesan. A beautiful young woman with blue eyes, blonde, and slim. Armand seduces her to make Marguerite suffer. Olympe has a futile and self-serving character. She understands that Armand seduces her to make Marguerite suffer, and she redoubles her malice towards Marguerite to please Armand. In contrast, Olympe, a courtesan like Marguerite, brings out the nobility and goodness of Marguerite.

KEYS TO READING

THE TRUE STORY OF MARIE DUPLESSIS

The Lady of the Camellias is a novel. However, it is based on real characters and a true story. The author announces this at the beginning of the novel:

> *"Not being yet old enough to invent, I am content to tell. I therefore urge the reader to be convinced of the reality of this story, in which all the characters, with the exception of the heroine, are still living"* (p.17).

Marguerite Gautier is in fact the avatar of a real-life courtesan, Marie Duplessis. Alexandre Dumas fils, the author of this book, was her lover. *The Lady of the Camellias* is about Alexandre Dumas fils' love for Marie Duplessis, but not all the events in the novel correspond to the real love story. For example, Alexandre Dumas fils and Marie Duplessis never had an idyllic love affair in Bougival, like Armand and Marguerite in the novel. In fact, the love story between Alexandre Dumas fils and Marie Duplessis was much less glorious than the one described in the novel, if one is to believe the commentators. As in the novel, Alexandre Dumas fils met Marie Duplessis for the first time in the Place de la Bourse, where he was struck by her beauty. He approached her a few years later, in 1844, at the Théâtre des Variétés. Their relationship ended in 1845 after an argument. Alexandre Dumas fils wrote to her: "My dear Marie, I am not rich enough to love you as I would like, nor poor enough to be loved as you would like. Let us therefore both forget, you a name which must be indifferent to you, I a happiness which is becoming impossible for me." Alexandre Dumas fils transcribes this letter as it stands in the novel, when Armand breaks up with Marguerite for the first time (p. 134).

Following this letter, Marie Duplessis became the lover of the Hungarian composer and pianist Franz Liszt. Like Marguerite, she also died of tuberculosis in Paris in February 1847, while Alexandre Dumas fils was travelling in Marseille. Dumas wrote *La Dame aux Camélias* in a month. The book was published in 1848. Armand's father does not correspond to Alexandre Dumas fils' father either, since Alexandre Dumas was known for his dissolute life and loose morals.

In the novel, Alexandre Dumas fils splits into two: he becomes the interlocutor of his character, Armand Duval, who nevertheless embodies the author in the same way that Marguerite Gautier embodies Marie Duplessis. In this respect, it should be noted that the character Armand Duval and his author share the same initials: A.D., proof that Alexandre Dumas fils was well aware of the literary process he was employing.

REALISM AND SOCIAL CRITICISM

A Realistic Novel

The Lady of the Camellias is often regarded as a precursor of the realist novel. Indeed, the emergence of realism in literature is usually dated from 1850, after the coup d'état of Napoleon III. This literary trend set itself the goal of describing the social reality of the time and the individuals: it must be as faithful a reproduction of reality as possible. Fictional and heroic themes are abandoned in favour of social description: realism evokes work, the growing importance of money in 19th century society, and love relationships. The realist novel, since it describes reality, also has a philosophical aim. Indeed, we will see later that the work of Alexandre Dumas fils has a moralizing function. Among the most important authors who belong to this movement, we can count Honoré de Balzac (1799-1850), Gustave Flaubert (1821-1880) and George Sand (1804-1876), a close friend of Alexandre Dumas fils. This trend then gave rise to naturalism, whose leader, Émile Zola (1840-1902), described the working-class conditions of his time. Finally, it should be noted that these literary currents had a great influence on the history of ideas, since they paved the way for the emergence of French sociology, founded by Émile Durkheim (French sociologist, 1858-1917) at the end of the 19th century. *The Lady of the Camellias* corresponds to certain criteria of the realist movement, since the author gives a precise description of the social milieu in Paris and the living conditions of courtesans.

 HISTORICAL CONTEXT

La Dame aux Camélias was published at a turbulent time in French history: until 1848, France lived under the monarchy of King Louis-Philippe. On 23 February

1848 (the year the novel was published, one year after the death of Marie Duplessis) a revolution established the Second Republic. But this did not last long, since on 2 December 1851, Napoleon III took power in a coup d'état and established the Second Empire.

A Social Critique

In *The Lady of the Camellias*, Alexandre Dumas fils does more than describe the life of courtesans and the bourgeois milieu of his time. There is a real social critique that runs through the whole book. First of all, the author denounces the bourgeois hypocrisy of kept women. He does this at the beginning of the book by mocking the curiosity of respectable women, who take advantage of Marguerite Gautier's death and the auctioning of her possessions to visit her home and learn more about these courtesans whom they rub shoulders with daily in theatres and opera houses: 'The one in whose house I was staying was dead; the most virtuous women could therefore enter her room' (p21). Later, the author continues his criticism through the scene in the cemetery: he talks to the gardener who explains that some bourgeois families, on learning that Marguerite Gautier was buried next to their forebears, had complained and demanded that the corpse be moved. The gardener does not fail to point out to the narrator that these families never visit the graves of their relatives and do not maintain them. Through this anecdote, the hypocrisy of bourgeois values is denounced. The whole story of Marguerite Gautier in the novel also serves to rehabilitate the image of the courtesan. Marguerite Gautier shows a moral strength and generosity of spirit that is lacking in all the characters around her: in the other courtesans, of course, but also and above all in the counts, dukes, nobles and rich people who are her lovers, in M. Duval, Armand's father, and in her friends. In *La Dame aux camélias*, the courtesan has more virtues than the nobles who buy the enjoyment of her beauty, before she grows old and is abandoned to her fate like Prudence Duvernoy. Marguerite Gautier, a courtesan though she may be, is capable of deep and total love. More than that, she aspires to happiness: hers first, but also Armand's and even that of M. Duval and his daughter, whom she does not know. Yet she is denied this happiness in the name of bourgeois moral values of respectability. Armand himself finds it difficult to understand and love her, because of her sulphurous past.

THE RECEPTION AND IMPACT OF THE WORK

La Dame aux Camélias was a great success when it was first published and had a major impact. Alexandre Dumas fils immediately had it adapted for the theatre, but it was initially censored as immoral. Finally, thanks to a change of minister, it was performed for the first time in 1852 at the Vaudeville Theatre. It was a phenomenal success, to the point of eclipsing the book. On the evening of the premiere, the Italian composer Giuseppe Verdi (1813-1901) was present. *The Lady of the Camellias* was a great inspiration to him, even though he too was involved in love affairs that were considered scandalous and which his father tried to oppose. It was on the basis of *The Lady of the Camellias* that Verdi composed his famous opera *La Traviata* in 1853. The novel was subsequently adapted many times in different artistic forms. At least fifteen films were inspired more or less directly by the work from 1907, with the first film adaptation by Viggo Larsen, to the present day (Baz Luhrman's *Moulin Rouge*, released in 2001, was inspired by the novel). The play has also been adapted several times and several ballet pieces have been created based on the novel. The character of Marguerite Gautier has had a worldwide impact, and has even inspired some Argentine tangos such as *Margarita Gautier* or *Margo*.

Despite the book's great impact and its enthusiastic reception at the time of publication, the author of *La Dame aux Camélias* was often criticised by his contemporaries. At a time when the realist movement was predominant, many writers reproached him for his pronounced taste for bon mots, witticisms and figures of speech. Rémy de Gourmont (French writer, 1858-1915) wrote in 1896: "Alexandre Dumas fils is not a great writer" (p. 270), while Émile Zola commented in 1876: "I do not like the talent of M. Alexandre Dumas fils. He is an extremely overrated writer, with a mediocre style and a conception shrunken by the strangest theories. I think that posterity will be hard on him" (*OEuvres complètes*, Vol. XII, p627). In view of the very many adaptations of *La Dame aux camélias*, it is clear that Emile Zola was wrong on this point. One can assume that some of these criticisms were not only motivated by literary reasons. Thus Léon Bloy (French novelist and essayist,

1846-1917) said: 'This mulatto... was a fool and a hypocrite' (p.270). This openly racist remark (*mulatto* being a word constructed from 'mule' which referred to people of mixed race during the colonial period) refers to Alexandre Dumas fils' origins. Like his father, he was the descendant of a slave in Saint-Domingue (present-day Haiti, a former French colony) who had had a child by her master.

AVENUES FOR REFLECTION

A FEW QUESTIONS FOR FURTHER REFLECTION...

* Why can we say that *La Dame aux Camélias* is part of the realist movement?

* In what way does the author take the side of the courtesans of his time?

* What motivated Armand to separate from Marguerite Gautier several times?

* What motivated Marguerite Gautier to leave Armand?

* Why does Marguerite Gautier stand out from other courtesans?

* What does the character of Prudence Duvernoy tell us about the living conditions of courtesans?

* Is Armand wrong to be jealous?

* What does the novel tell us about life in Paris in the mid-1900s?

TO GO FURTHER

REFERENCE EDITION

DUMAS A. fils, *La Dame aux camélias*, Le Livre de poche, 1975.

BENCHMARK STUDIES

LIVIO, A. *Preface and comments* (included in the reference edition) Le Livre de poche, 1975.

ADDITIONAL SOURCES

PRÉVOST, A.F. *Manon Lescaut*, 1731

ADAPTATIONS

VERDI, G. *La Traviata*. 1853, opera.

DUMAS, A. *La Dame aux camélias*, 1852, play.

DE CECCATTY, R. *La Dame aux camélias*, 2000, play.

LARSEN, V. *The Lady of the Camellias*, 1907, film.

CUKOR, G. *Le roman de Marguerite Gautier*, 1936, cinema.

SAUGET, H. *La Dame aux camélias*, 1957, ballet.

LEFEBRE, J. *La Dame aux camélias*, 1980, ballet.

Your opinion is important to us!
Leave a comment on the website of your online bookshop
and share your favourites on social networks!

Ebook EAN: 9782808686563
Paperback EAN: 9782808697965
Legal Deposit: D/2023/12603/1076

Cover: © Primento
Digital conception by Primento, the digital partner of publishers.